I0726118

Books by P. J. Hoover

Interactive Adventures
Deadly Decisions: Into the Woods
Pick Your Own Quest Series (written as Connor Hoover)

Write Your Own Quest: The Ultimate Guide to Writing Your Own Interactive Adventure

Anthologies
Castle of Horror: Volume 1
Castle of Horror: Holiday Horrors
Castle of Horror: Summer Lovin'
Castle of Horror: Femme Fatales (editor)
Castle of Horror: Love Gone Wrong
Castle of Horror: Saturday Mournings

Novels
Furiously Awesome
Solstice
A Broken Truce
A Ruined Land
A Buried Spark
The Hidden Code

DEADLY DECISIONS

INTO THE WOODS

BY
P. J. HOOVER

ROOTS IN MYTH, AUSTIN, TX

Deadly Decisions: Into the Woods

Deadly Decisions is part of the
Pick Your Own Quest™ brand.

Pick Your Own Quest™ is a registered
trademark of Roots in Myth

A Root in Myth Book
Austin, Texas
For more information, write
pjhoover@pjhoover.com
www.pjhoover.com

Paperback ISBN: 978-1-949717-35-8

To Alec, for your
constant support

You've seen the movies. Five teenagers venture into a haunted house on a dare. Only one of them comes out alive. The others die horrible grizzly deaths, each while trying to get to safety. Except in their attempts to escape, they do the exact opposite of what they should do. They go down the dark hall. They open the trapdoor under the carpet. They dare to look behind the coats in the spooky closet. You scream at them. You tell them not to do it. And yet they do. And they die. If only they had listened.

Good news. Now it's your chance. You get to make the choices. You get to try to stay alive. No more bad decisions. I know you'll do great. Here's one thing to keep in mind though. In the movie, four out of five don't make it out alive. The odds are against you. You've been warned. Also, what if the only way to safety is down through the trapdoor . . . ?

Are you ready to test your survival skills? Great! Try not to die.

If you dare, turn the page.

It's been four years since you've seen your best pals from high school. Four years since the graduation that sent you on your own separate paths. That broke up the gang. Joey went to college in Colorado for engineering. You're pretty sure he's got a big-time job lined up with some oil company, but he's a little vague about it. Hannah went to Texas, graduated, and is about to go to med school. Last you heard, she wants to be an oncologist and help little kids who have cancer. James went to trade school and now works at the Land Rover dealership, fixing rich people's cars all day long. Claire? You have no idea what Claire's been doing for the last four years. Nothing if you had to guess. Pretty much like what she did in high school. And you? Well, you're not setting the world on fire with all you've accomplished, but life's been pretty good so far. So good, actually, that you decided it was the perfect time to plan a get together over the long weekend with your best old pals.

Joey and you fly in at about the same time, and while you're waiting for the others, you grab a beer at the airport bar. Pretty soon you're laughing about the time you dared him to eat an entire pack of hotdogs the same night he'd done seven shots of vodka. The results were not pretty. Now it's hilarious. At the time . . . not so much. You'd had a hard time eating hotdogs for a good six months.

Hannah texts you when she lands, and she meets you two at the bar. Then it's another two hours before James and Claire arrive. You, Joey, and Hannah have had way too many drinks to drive, and Claire's eyes are really red, so James gets elected to drive the rental van. Also, he is the car guy, so it makes sense.

The five of you pile in, then after a quick stop at the grocery, you're heading toward the Shenandoah Mountains to go camping. Once off the Interstate, the scenery around you changes. No more office buildings and strip malls. There are trees and mountains and farms and a whole lot of nothing else.

"Hey, stop for that guy," Joey says as you pass a hitchhiker.

"No way," Hannah says. "You should never pick up hitchhikers. A friend of a friend picked up a hitchhiker one time, and turned out he was an escaped convict."

"A friend of a friend!" James laughs. "Ha!"

"What's so funny about that?" Hannah asks.

"That's how all urban legends start," James says. "It's not real."

You're pretty sure you've heard the same urban legend, so you agree with James, and then ask when you can pull over to take a piss. Maybe you shouldn't have had that fourth beer. Or was it a fifth?

"We're almost there," James says.

You hope you can hold it that long.

"I know a crazy ghost story that's real," Claire says, her eyes all serious. "It's about this little girl who went missing in these mountains." She gestures at the mountain range off to the left. "Her parents decided they didn't want her anymore. They were horrible, awful people. They brought her out here to the mountains and left her in the woods. They went home, had a few drinks, some crap ass sex, and a good night's sleep. When they woke up, they changed their minds. They came back looking for her, but they never found her. And then they went missing. Rumor has it that she fell into a deep pit in a cave and couldn't get out. And if you go into the cave, late at night, you can still hear her calling for help. And if you aren't careful . . ."

"What?" you ask. Chills run up your arms.

Claire shrugs. "I don't know. I can't remember the rest. I guess she eats you or something."

"A little ghost girl eats you?" James said. "That makes no sense."

Joey pushes his head forward from the far back of the van. "You know why my parents would never let me go camping out here during high school?"

Hannah laughs. "Because they were crazy overprotective?"

It's true. Joey was the one who always had to be home by midnight, even on graduation night. Not like that kept him from partying. He just couldn't let his parents know.

"Well, that," Joey says. "But it's also because of the Satanic cult."

"What Satanic cult?" you ask.

"The one that lives here in the mountains," Joey says. "My parents said they use the sacred ground of the mountains for their human sacrifices and that they prey upon the weak."

James shakes his head. "Man, ghosts and satanic cults. You guys are crazy, you know that."

"Just a little drunk," Joey says.

"That too," James says. He takes a left turn onto a dirt road, then turns up the radio. The news comes on, talking about how a patient escaped from a nearby insane asylum.

"That could have been the hitchhiker!" Hannah says.

In no universe would you ever pick up a hitchhiker, so you should be okay.

As James winds his way along the dirt path, the stories continue. The Twisted Twins—two serial killer brothers who peel the skin from their victims and make lampshades out of them. The Ghostly Gravedigger—a deranged undertaker who buries his victims alive. The Meat Hook Maniac—a former meat factory worker who is rumored to still roam the factory and stock the meat cellar with dead bodies.

The five of you are chatting and laughing just like in high school. It's like no time has passed at all. This is going to be the best camping trip ever. Three days reliving the good old days. Then you can each go your separate ways and grow up and do whatever boring grown-up people do.

James is using GPS to get to the campsite, but it cuts out after you pass through a valley. By now, your buzz is starting to wear off. It's a good thing you bought a bunch more beer at the grocery.

"Don't worry, I know the way," James says. "It's just on the other side of the bridge."

Sure enough, about five minutes ahead is a rickety bridge, and not far beyond that, through the woods, is a clearing.

"Viola!" James says. "I told you I knew the way."

Great. Now you can finally piss. You head off in the woods, trying not to think about the stupid urban legends your friends were telling. They aren't real. Woods are just nature, and there is nothing scary about that.

When you get back to camp, Claire is smoking, Joey and Hannah each have a beer, and James is staring at his cell phone.

"There's no signal out here," James says.

The rest of you check your phones. He's right. No signal.

"Like not even emergency calls?" you ask.

"Like nothing," James says.

"It's like we're living in the 1980s!" Hannah says. "Let's get this party started!"

Claire and Joey decide they're going to collect firewood. James and Hannah offer to stay at camp and set up everyone's tents. You actually get a feeling they're going to be sharing a tent, based on the way James keeps accidentally brushing up against Hannah every chance he gets. Also, she's laughing at all his jokes, which aren't that funny.

You aren't sure you want to expend the energy collecting firewood, but if you stay here at camp, you might feel like a third wheel.

If you help Claire and Joey collect firewood, turn to page 11.

If you stay at the campsite and help set up the tents, turn to page 8.

Setting up tents isn't the best fun ever, but it has to be done. Also, it's better than lugging around a bunch of firewood. James sets up his tent first.

"Hey, can you help me with something inside my tent?" James says to Hannah.

She giggles and disappears inside and . . . well . . . yeah, you wish you'd thought to pack earplugs. But whatever. You grab a beer from the cooler and get to work setting up your tent on the opposite side of the firepit. Whatever they're doing, they are taking forever.

Okay, you know what they're doing. You're not stupid. Hopefully, it'll just be quick. You lay out the tarps for Joey's tent on one side of yours and Claire's tent on the other. Just as you're unrolling Joey's tent to set it up, Hannah and James come out of his tent.

"Don't do all the work without us," James says.

And Hannah laughs.

You should have gone and collected firewood instead.

"And don't drink all the beer," Hannah says and grabs one for herself from the cooler.

Between the three of you, the remaining three tents are up in fifteen minutes . . . more than enough time to finish your beer and start on another.

"How come Joey and Claire aren't back?" James says.

They have been gone for like an hour now. How hard can it be to find firewood? Also, the sun's about to set, and you can't remember if they brought flashlights or not.

"Maybe you should go look for them?" Hannah says. You notice how she doesn't offer to go.

"Yeah, maybe," James says. He tosses the keys to the minivan into his tent and grabs a flashlight. "If I'm not back in fifteen minutes, send help."

Hannah giggles, then winks, and you fight the urge to roll your eyes. Then James slips through the trees and out of sight. That leaves you and Hannah.

"Oh, the stakes!" you say. "We need to stake down the tents." Sure, it's not windy now, but there's nothing worse than having your tent blow around you while you're inside.

You grab two rubber mallets, handing one to Hannah. "You stake down yours and James's, and I'll do these three."

The ground is soft, and the stakes go in easy. You step around your tent to drive the last spike into the ground when you hear something that sounds a lot like crying.

"Hello?" you call out softly.

The crying stops.

Weird.

Then it begins, but softer this time, almost like a whisper on the wind. A chill pushes through you. What if there is someone out there? They could be hurt? It could be Joey or Claire.

"Hey, come see this!" Hannah calls, interrupting your thoughts. "This is crazy." She sounds far away.

If you investigate the crying sound, turn to page 2o.

If you see what Hannah is talking about, turn to page 14.

Being a third wheel is like the opposite of fun. You learned that at senior prom when Claire and . . . whoever that douche bag she was dating at the time . . . insisted you come along. "We'll have a great time!" she'd said. Yeah, no. The great time ended as soon as they started sucking face in the backseat while you drove.

"I'll help you guys collect firewood," you say. You're pretty sure Claire and Joey aren't planning on hooking up.

"Far out," Claire says. It's about the tenth time she's said it in the last forty-five minutes. Far out is where you guys are. Far out, away from civilization. Ah, nature is bliss.

In your mind you have an idea what collecting firewood will be like. You'll walk around and come across perfect branches that stack neatly. Turns out this isn't reality at all. You look everywhere, but it's like someone has raked the whole place. There's not a stick to be found.

"Hey, guys," you say. "I'm going to head over there to look."

Joey cranes his neck to see where you're pointing. "Over in that deep, dark area of the forest?" he says. "No way. Not me."

"I don't mind going alone," you say. Nature is not scary. Well, bears are scary, but what are the odds of you stumbling across a grizzly bear?

"Far out," Claire says and sinks down, back against a tree. "I'm gonna sit here and convene with nature."

"Commune with nature," you say.

"Yeah, that," Claire says.

"I have an idea for how to get firewood," Joey says. "We can use a lever and pulley system and . . ."

You tune him out after that and head off to find all the firewood. And yeah, Joey was right about one thing. This part of the forest is really dark. The trees are packed close together and shadows follow your every movement. You pull out your cell phone and turn on the flashlight, but that only makes the shadows move more, which, you can't lie, freaks you out a bit.

"There are no bears," you say to yourself. Then you hear a growl.

It's your stomach. The potato skins you had at the bar must've gone through your system, probably from the copious amount of grease. If only you'd thought to bring some snacks along. Or Tums.

The sound of your growling stomach is interrupted by a scream. It sounds like Joey!

"Joey?" you call.

No answer.

"Claire?"

Nothing. They should be able to hear you from here. You call again, but they're not answering, and you start to get worried. Maybe Joey's lever and pulley system collapsed on him and he's getting crushed by a tree branch right now.

You take off running, back the way you came. But the forest is so dark, and you can't find Claire or Joey or the campsite. Oh wait! There's a light. It flickers and glows. That's got to be them. They must've gotten the fire started. You run toward the light, but when the trees open up, there is a vast wide space ahead of you. It's an old cemetery, and the graves are glowing. That's definitely not the campsite. You dash back into the woods and take another path. This one brings you out at the edge of a cornfield. Cornstalks rustle in the wind. Not the campsite either. You hurry back into the woods.

There's another scream. You can't tell if it's coming from the cemetery or the cornfield.

"Joey? Claire?" You barely whisper their names.

Still nothing. And you know you need to help your friends. But are they in the cemetery or the cornfield?

If you head to the cemetery, turn to page 18.

If the cornfield is a much better idea, turn to page 22.

The crying must have been your overactive imagination. There is nobody out here except you and your friends. Also, it's dark, and you don't want to go off into the woods alone.

"Hannah?" you call.

"Over here," she yells back. Her voice sounds far away. Guess she wasn't afraid to wander off in the dark. And since you haven't seen her in four years, you don't want her thinking you're scared. Still, a little light would be a stellar idea. You scramble around camp real quick, looking for a flashlight, but can't find one. Whatever. You can always use your cell phone for light, even with no reception. You're pretty sure you have at least half battery.

"Where are you?" you yell back.

"This way," she calls.

You head in the direction you think her voice is coming from, pushing into the trees and low brush. It scrapes at your arms and face, but you've walked enough in the woods to not get cut up. You call her name four more times. Each time she answers, it sounds closer. At least you're heading in the right direction. Finally, you push through the trees and come out into a clearing.

There stands Hannah at the end of a long dirt driveway. And at the other end of the driveway is a cabin set back against the trees.

You hurry up to her and stop. "Whoa. Who lives here?" you ask. It's got shutters over every window, but half of them are barely held on by a hinge. The front steps have shifted so they're aligned at an angle, like some fun house at a carnival. It looks like at one point the cabin may have been painted brown, but there are large flaked-off areas showing dull wood beneath. And worst of all, it's dark, like it's being swallowed by shadows.

"No idea," Hannah says. "But James isn't back yet, and I wonder if he went in here."

If James went into this creepy-ass looking cabin alone, then he deserves whatever horrible fate awaits him. This place looks like something out of a horror movie.

"Let's go in," Hannah says and skips a couple steps forward.

You grab her wrist. "Are you kidding?"

She shakes her wrist free. "It's fine."

"It's not," you say. "This is the kind of place serial killers live." You remember the story of the Twisted Twins. This was probably their birth home.

"Don't be such a baby," Hannah says. "The worst that's going to happen is James is inside and he's going to jump out and scare us."

So, against your better judgment, you follow Hannah up the driveway to the cabin, and up the rickety steps. When you take the last step, the front door creaks and swings open about a foot.

Hannah smiles and points at it. Then she mouths, "James."

Before you can stop her, she pushes the door open all the way and jumps forward and says, "Boo!"

Silence and darkness are the only response. There is no sign of James. There is no sign of anyone. You get a really bad feeling in the pit of your stomach.

"Let's go back to camp," you say. Sitting by the fire, roasting a marshmallow and drinking a beer sounds perfect just about now.

16

"Let's check it out," Hannah says, and she steps inside . . . which leaves you on the porch alone. You step in after her.

The cabin is not large. Downstairs, there is a room on either side with a staircase in the middle. On the side of the staircase is a door that can't lead to any other rooms based on the layout.

You point at it. "That probably leads down to a cellar."

Hannah's eyes go wide. "Oh cool. We should split up. I'll check out the cellar and you go see what's upstairs."

Splitting up is not a good idea. But creepy cellars aren't a good idea either.

If you split up and go check out the upstairs alone, turn to page 24.

If you stay together and brave the cellar, turn to page 36.

There's no way Joey or Claire would have gone into a cornfield. Those places are the things of nightmares. So, the cemetery it is. You take the path that leads back to the glowing cemetery, and then you cover the fifty feet to where the graves begin. It's impossible that the graves are glowing, but there's no denying it. You work it out in your mind. It's probably some kind of algae stuck on the headstones that's reflecting the moonlight. You walk closer to one of the graves and brush your hand over the stone.

A weird shock runs through you, which has got to be nerves because yours are stretched pretty tight right now. But if it is algae, it doesn't rub off. You bend close to read the words engraved there.

Stanley, age 11, died 1904

The next graves you come across are similar. All young boys, no older than thirteen, all died in 1904. And then you remember a story your mom told you once. She'd gone to college out near here, and she said back in 1904 there had been a horrible factory fire. The factory used kids as cheap labor, beating them and exposing them to toxic fumes and horrible work conditions. One day, some of the kids rebelled. A canister of chemicals got knocked over and caught fire. And because the kids were locked in, everyone died.

Almost as soon as the story plays out in your mind, you begin to hear low moans. The ghosts of the kids. Your teeth start chattering, and you really wish you hadn't decided to look for firewood alone.

You step back from the grave and scan the cemetery, trying to ignore the moaning voices. It's got to be the wind . . . except you've never heard wind like that before. If Joey or Claire had come here, where would they be?

There! You spot it. At the center of the cemetery is a crypt. Like the rest of the graves, it's glowing. And the grate that covers the door looks like it's hanging open. Joey or Claire could be in there. You should go check it out. But a voice inside your head also tells you that this is a horrible idea.

If you check out the crypt, turn to page 30.

If you get as far away from the crypt as possible, turn to page 40.

"Just a second!" you call to Hannah. She doesn't respond, so you hope she hears you.

Then you listen again, being very silent. You don't hear the crying at first, but then, there it is, floating on the wind. What if someone really needs help? It could even be Claire. Maybe something happened while collecting firewood.

"Hello?" you whisper.

Again, there's no answer, but the crying continues. You step into the trees, following the sound. Shadows seem to press around you. You can't tell if they're trying to push you away or push you forward. The crying never falls in pitch. It stays steady as you move through the woods. And when you step out from the trees and find yourself right next to the mountain, you know you've found the source.

In front of you is a cave. A dark cave. It's not like some cave that you've seen in a movie, with a perfect elliptical opening high enough for you to just walk right through. Instead, it's barely four feet tall. The edges are uneven, and the stone overhanging the top looks like it could topple at any second.

"Hello?" you whisper again.

Whoever is crying, it's coming from inside the cave.

"Claire?" you call.

No answer. But the crying sounds like a young girl.

You want the crying to be your imagination, because the last thing you want to do is go into this small, dark cave. But you also know that if someone is inside there, you need to help them. Still, if that rock falls while you're inside, you're going to be trapped in there forever. Maybe there's another entrance. A bigger opening that doesn't look like one inconvenient sneeze would be your end.

If you go into the cave through this small opening, turn to page 28.

If you search around for a bigger, better opening to the cave, turn to page 38.

There's another scream. It sounds like Claire for sure this time, and there is no doubt it's coming from the cornfield. Man, when you find Claire, you're going to have some serious words with her about not wandering off alone, especially into some stupid cornfield. What was she thinking?

You've never walked in a cornfield before, but in your mind, it goes like this. As long as you pick a row of corn and follow it, you should never get lost. Easy peasy. You cross the short distance to the cornfield and go in.

Here's the reality. No sooner are you ten steps in, in the dark, you've completely lost your way. Every stalk of corn looks the same as the next, almost like they've been genetically engineered to grow identical to each other.

You stop walking and wait for Claire to scream again. But the only sound you hear is the wind rustling through the cornstalks. You turn around, because maybe it's time to head back the way you came. Except you're really smart about it. You keep one foot pointed in the direction you're facing and then you turn your body back the other way, like some crazy game of Twister. You count to ten. One . . . two . . . three . . .

At eight, a scream pierces the silence. It's Claire, and it's coming from up ahead. You have to go deeper into the corn. You walk for ten minutes. There is no sign of Claire. No sign of anything. And with each step you take, you know you should turn back. You can get the rest of your friends. Maybe find the farmer who owns this land. Then you can come back all together and find Claire. Except if you have to be honest, you don't trust that you've walked consistently in a straight line.

Think think think. Back when you were looking out over the cornfield, there was a scarecrow deep in the middle. If you can find the scarecrow, you can climb the pole and see what direction you need to head. But it also seemed like there was some kind of path cut through the corn off to the right. If you could find the path, it could lead you out of here.

If you look for the scarecrow, turn to page 33.

If you look for a path, turn to page 42.

You know that splitting up is not a good idea, but neither is a creepy cellar. And let's face it. Hannah is kind of a liability. All she's worried about is finding James so they can go back to his tent and . . .

Now that you think about it, back in high school, they'd always get drunk and hook up at parties. Her being off in Texas has probably put a damper on that. And it's not like you're jealous. If the two of them want to spend the entire camping trip like a couple of bunny rabbits, that just means more beer for you.

"Be careful," you say, but Hannah is already hurrying ahead and prying the door open.

You start up the stairs, holding your cell phone out in front of you so the light shines on the wooden steps. The first step you take, the wood makes a creaking sound so loud you're sure it would wake the dead. The second step is worse. And the third step, your foot goes through.

"Shit!" you shout, and you drop your cell phone. The light goes out. "Shit!" you say again, then you fumble and pick it up. The screen is cracked. You try to slide your finger on it to turn the flashlight back on, but the flashlight is screwed. So instead, you use the screen to light up the stairs.

You're up about seven steps when you hear a rhythmic creaking sound coming from upstairs. Maybe it is

James. But no way are you going to let him scare you. If anything, you're going to scare the piss out of him. That would serve him right for leaving you and Hannah alone.

You reach the top of the steps and find yourself in a hallway. There is a room down to the left, a room down to the right, and a room ahead. You hold your breath and listen to the creaking. It seems to be coming from the left.

You tiptoe along the wooden floor, keeping to the sides so the boards creaking won't be quite so bad. The rhythmic creaking coming from the room gets louder and louder. Crick. Creak. Crick. Creak. You move forward, so silent that you're barely breathing. And then you're at the door to the room.

The moon shines through a window, lighting the space up enough that you can see a rocking chair with its back to you. It rocks back and forth. Back and forth. Whoever is in the chair, they don't know you're here.

Okay, this has gone far enough. If this is James, then he's needs to grow up and stop trying to scare you.

"Hello?" you call in a loud whisper.

There's no answer.

"Hello?" you say again. Your heart is beating so loudly, that whoever is in that chair must hear it.

There's still no answer.

If you step into the room and see who's in the chair, turn to page 62.

If you back out of the room and get the hell out of here, turn to page 45.

Going into this cave is the only humane thing to do. You have to help this poor, lost child.

"I'm coming in," you call ahead, just so you don't startle anyone.

There's no answer. Then you get down on our hands and knees and scramble ahead, into the darkness. The amount of time it takes to go from dark to pitch black is instant. You wave your hand in front of your face, but can't see it. You test the height once inside, and find that you can stand. Then you pull your cell phone from your pocket and use the flashlight to light up the area around you.

The rock walls are dripping with moisture. The cave is deep, so much that you can't see the back of it. The crying persists, much louder now that you're actually inside the cave.

"Where are you?" you call. "I can help you."

Still no one answers.

"I'm coming," you call out. Then you move forward, into the dark of the cave. You stay away from the walls, but some drops do fall on your head. They're stickier than you would have thought, but it could just be the humidity. You trudge forward over the uneven ground, nearly twisting your ankle on rocks that get underfoot. Still the crying continues. It's only when you reach the back wall of the chamber you're in, that the crying stops.

You hold your breath. You don't make a sound. And instead of crying, a chirping sound begins. It's low at first, then it gets louder. And louder. No normal insect you can think of could make that sound.

If you turn around and leave, turn to page 50.

If you investigate the chirping sound, turn to page 68.

Y ou creep closer to the crypt, trying not to make a sound. The moaning of the voices is getting louder, almost as if it's coming from not all the graves but from this one big crypt.

Engraved letters begin to take shape as you get closer, and even though you're about to pee your pants, you still want to see who's buried here. If all these little kids are in these graves, then who would be important enough to have this kind of fancy monument? It's got to be at least six feet tall and has columns and carvings. There's even a gargoyle on either side of the marble rooftop. The engraving says:

Samuel Phillips
Phillips Chemical Company
Died 1904

No way. This must be the grave of the guy who owned the factory. How dare he be given such a fancy place to lay to rest when he was directly responsible for the death of all these poor helpless kids? Anger mixes with the fear that runs through you.

A scream breaks you from your thoughts. Okay, there is no mistaking it this time. That is Joey. And the scream came from inside the crypt.

Against every bit of common sense rattling around in your brain, you pull on the metal grate that covers the opening.

It's locked. You yank hard. Still, it doesn't give. You want to call out to Joey, to tell him you're coming, but if someone is in there with him, you don't want to let them know you're here.

You turn, looking for something you can use to pry open the grate, but then you hear a creaking sound behind you. Slowly, you turn to look.

The grate is open.

"No big deal," you say to yourself. You must've unstuck it and just not realized it. And now that it's open, you have no choice but to go inside. Deep breath. You step in.

There are two shelves on either side of you, and on each is a stone coffin. It must be the Phillips guy and his family. In the center of the small space is an urn. But other than that, there is no sign of Joey.

You grab the urn as you move around it, but the moment you touch it, it slides to the side, revealing a secret passageway with stairs leading down.

"Run!" you think, but you're not the kind of friend who's going to leave their buddy in the lurch. So even though your brain is literally screaming at you to turn around and dash away, you start down the stairs.

The moaning is getting way louder. And with the moaning is chanting. A bunch of voices all chanting words that sound like they're in some other language. Once you reach the bottom of the stairs, you coming to an opening. Ahead is a large chamber filled with dozens of people. They're dressed in robes, some red and some black. There are large pentagrams drawn everywhere, dripping red like they're painted in blood. And at the center of the group is a table.

Strapped to the table is Joey!

He's naked and even from this far away, you can see the fear in his eyes. You need to help him!

If you look for one of the robes to put on so you can try to blend in while you save him, turn to page 54.

If you go back and try to find your other friends so they can help, turn to page 72.

If you just start heading off and changing directions, you are going to get miserably lost. You can't let that happen. Of course, you wouldn't starve to death. You could eat all the corn in the world. Wait, can people eat raw corn? You'll have to remember to search it on the internet when you get cell phone coverage again. Anyway, the best thing to do is to look for the scarecrow.

You look up, trying to use the moon as your guide. It's a little ahead of you, high in the sky. You think that means it's south. Not that you're sure what to do with that information.

Screw it. You keep walking the way you were walking. You trust your inner gut. And then there it is. The scarecrow pole! Best part? There are small little rungs on it, like a ladder, making it easier to climb.

You look up. "Oh, hello there, Mr. Scarecrow," you say. Yes, it's dorky, but you're just really freaking glad you found it.

The scarecrow doesn't answer.

"Claire!" you call out, cupping your hands around your mouth. "Claire! Where are you?"

Around you is only the echo of your voice carrying on the wind.

You grab hold of the first rung and lift your foot. Then you look up again.

The scarecrow is pointing a different way. Thirty seconds ago, it was looking off to the left. Now it's looking off to the right. You're not wrong. You know it.

Maybe it's on some kind of pivot and the wind makes it turn automatically. Yeah, that would make sense. That would explain how it's facing the complete opposite direction than it was. If Joey were here, he'd probably go on and on explaining the whole pivot thing. Or maybe you did imagine it and it didn't change direction. Maybe you are wrong.

From this angle, you get a good look at the scare-crow's face. It's terrifying. Like you think back to the scariest scarecrow you ever saw, which was in some Batman movie, and this is like a gazillion times worse.

Its face is made of a burlap sack, but there are dark splotches covering the cheeks. The eyes look like gaping pits, and if you didn't know better, you'd say they were filled with the fires of hell. Its mouth is sewn in giant ragged stitches, like bad taxidermy. The clothes are in tatters, with straw sticking out everywhere.

You know, maybe you don't have to climb the scarecrow pole to get a better look. You could just wing it. Except now, with the whole changing direction thing, you have no idea which direction you even came from.

If you climb the scarecrow pole to get a better look, turn to page 58.

If you get as far away from this scarecrow as possible, turn to page 78.

No matter how creepy the cellar is, it's a way better idea to stay together.

"Want to check out the upstairs first?" you ask.

Hannah looks at you like you're crazy. "No way. We have to find James."

James is as likely upstairs as in the cellar, but Hannah's got her mind made up.

Together the two of you tread over to the door on the side of the stairwell. There are scrape marks on the floor, as if it's been opened recently.

You point at them. "You see that?" you whisper.

"James," she whispers back.

Maybe. Hopefully. Better James than some creepy serial killer.

You reach forward and twist the knob. It turns easily as if it's been oiled. And then you pull the door open. It swings across the floor, creating a small cloud of dust.

"You first," you say. This was Hannah's idea, so if there is something down there, better for her to be the one to die. Not that she's going to die. That's like something out of a horror movie. Okay, this whole thing is like something out of a horror movie.

Hannah leads the way, and you follow. And once down in the basement, you shine your cell phone flashlight around. Then you wish you hadn't.

The whole place looks like some kind of murder basement. There are hooks on walls and tables with knives and pliers. And there are stains that you really hope are ink but you're sure are blood. Also, there's no one around.

"James isn't here. Can we leave now?" you ask.

But no sooner are the words out of your mouth, the door to the cellar slams shut. You and Hannah look at each other. Her eyes are wide.

You dash up the stairs and push at the door. It won't budge. It was perfectly oiled, meaning it must be locked. Shit. This is not good.

You hurry back downstairs. By now, Hannah is crying.

"We're never going to get out of here," she blubbers.

Her crying is not helping the situation at all. She's useless. Meaning it's up to you to find a way out. The way you see it, you have two options. You could try to break the door down, or you could look for an alternate way out. Lots of old cellars have back entrances that lead directly outside.

If you try to break down the door, turn to page 48.

If you look for a back exit, turn to page 64.

You want to help, but going through this opening will be your end. So, instead, you move off to the side, looking for another entrance. The crying fades, and you worry you're going to lose it altogether. But also, maybe you imagined the entire thing. Wait. It looks like there's a plateau up above the cave. You're no spelunker, but from what you remember about the times you've gone hiking, sometimes there are openings on flat areas that cavers can then rappel into. Not that you're going to rappel. You've had way too many beers, and you don't even have rope.

You climb up the side of the mountain until you get to the plateau. The crying stops altogether. You stand and listen just to make sure. Then a piercing scream breaks through the air! It's one of your friends, and they're calling your name! Shit, you have to help them.

You take off running, back down the hill and through the woods. You're doing the best you can with the moon lighting your path. You stumble a few times, but you avoid running into a tree. The screaming continues. You're almost there. Then, as you're running, something clamps around your ankle, biting into your flesh and bone.

"Ahhh!!" you shout, and you fall to the ground, your momentum carrying you forward and pulling on your ankle. You turn to see how bad it is. Moonlight reflects off metal. There's a giant bear trap latched onto your ankle. Blood pours out of the wounds, and you're sure you're going to get tetanus and die because there's so much rust on the thing.

You reach down and try to pry it off, but even the smallest movement puts you into excruciating pain.

Then you hear laughter, and someone says, "Looks like we got ourselves another one."

Shit. You look up toward the sound of the voice. Two silhouetted figures stand there on a ridge, backlit by the moon. They're looking right at you.

"Yup," the second voice says. "We best get down there and nab it."

Like hell you're going to let that happen. But what choice do you have? If you try to get the bear trap off yourself, the pain will be unbearable. If you stay here and let them get it off, then once it's off, you can attack them and run.

If you try to get the bear trap off though it means excruciating pain, turn to page 52.

If you wait for them to take it off then run, turn to page 70.

Maybe you aren't the smartest person in the world, but you do know that going into a creepy crypt in a creepy graveyard is not a good idea. Like in no world is that something you should do. What is a good idea is getting back to the campsite (where everybody else probably is, wondering where you are), kicking back with a beer, making s'mores over the campfire, and telling ghost stories.

Okay, maybe not ghost stories. Maybe just stupid jokes? Anyway, you can figure that out when you get there.

You turn around. Fog is rolling in over the entire cemetery, blanketing it. It glows slightly green, like the gravestones. And a chill runs through the air. You wrap your arms around yourself, push thoughts of the crypt far from your mind, and start trudging across the ground toward the trees.

You kick at least two gravestones. "Oops," you say, like the poor little dead kids buried there can hear you.

Wait, they can't hear you, can they? Do dead people hear?

Then you hear sounds, like the voices of children laughing. They're everywhere, all around you. And that's about all you can take. You run. You try to avoid the gravestones but you can't see the ground worth a shit. And then you take another step . . . and fall . . . about six feet down.

You're on your hands and knees, but you turn over. You've fallen into a rectangle dug into the earth.

An empty grave.

You should have opted for being the third wheel, because this is horrible. You scramble to stand up just as a silhouette of a person comes and stands over you. You can't see their face because the moon is casting them in shadows. But you can see that they're holding something long in their right hand, like a weapon.

"Anyone down there?" they call.

Wait, they can't see you. If you don't move, maybe they'll move on and then you can get out of here. But they'd still be out there, waiting for you. It may be better if you go ahead and try to attack them now.

If you **attack** the person, turn to page 75.

If you **don't** move, hoping they'll go away, turn to page 56.

Heading deeper into the cornfield to look for the scarecrow doesn't seem like a very good idea. What does seem like a good idea is looking for a path out of here. You trust your instincts and turn right, doing the best you can to make a solid 90-degree turn. Above, the moon slips behind a cloud. It's dark and getting darker by the second. Why did you come running off into this stupid cornfield in the first place?

Oh right, because Claire screamed, and what kind of friend would you be if you just ignored her? A smart friend but a bad friend, that's what kind. You try not to think about how much you wish you were back at the campsite right now. You'll find Claire. Find the path, and get back there.

Luck is on your side because ahead you see a gap in the corn. Success! You've found the path. You shine your cell phone flashlight ahead and step onto it. It's wide enough for two people and leads straight ahead . . . well, that is until you come to a fork in the path.

Left or right? Left or right? You decide on left. One is as good as another. You travel down the path, and a few minutes later, you come to another fork in the path. Left or right? Oh, you get it. You are in a corn maze!

You remember back to when you were a kid and your parents took you to a pumpkin farm around Halloween. The place bragged about having the biggest and most intricate corn maze in the state. But that thing was no problem for you. When you came out, five minutes later, your parents were amazed. In fact, you even had to go back in and save your little brother who was stuck and terrified in some dead end, sure the corn was going to eat him.

The good news? Corn doesn't eat people. You found your little brother and got him out. And . . . you know the secret to mazes! As long as you pick a direction and ALWAYS turn that way, you will find your way out. Bring it!

You backtrack just once to the first path you started on, and this time you go right. Then, every time you come to a fork in the path, you turn right. Right. Right. Right. You'll be out of here in no time.

Except an hour goes by. You still haven't found your way out. You keep at it, always heading to the right. Your brain tries to tell you to turn around, but if you do that, all the hard work you've put in for the last hour will be wasted, so you stick at it for another hour. Then a horrible thought floats into your mind. What if this corn maze is no maze at all? What if the path led to a giant square, and all you've been doing is going around and around the square? Just the thought makes you want to cry. And so you do something you know you shouldn't do. At the next intersection, you turn left. From off in the distance, someone giggles.

You whip around. There is no one there.

You follow the path down to the end, to the next intersection, and there, in the middle, against the corn, is a sign. Carved into the wood is a symbol—like a rune or something. You took a linguistics course back in college, and you're sure it looks familiar. You know you've seen this symbol before. And then it comes to you. You know this symbol. It's an ancient symbol for death. Another giggle. No way was that your imagination.

Okay, that's it. You need to get out of here. It seems like you have two choices. You could continue on, now taking the left and left and left, trying to find your way out of this stupid corn maze, or you could scrap the maze and push your way through the corn walls.

If you stick with the maze, turn to page 60.

If you push your way through the corn walls, turn to page 80.

You open your mouth, about to say "hello" once more, but screw that. You back out of the doorframe and back down the hall. What you'll do is find Hannah and get the hell out of here. The floorboards in the hallway squeak as you step on them. The more steps you take, the more a horrible feeling takes over you. Coming into this cabin was not a good idea.

When you get to the top of the staircase, the creaking of the rocking chair stops. Then there's a sound like it scraping across wood. Then a footstep.

Nope. You dash down the stairs, taking them two at a time. But you forget about the one you went through, and when your foot lands on it, you fall the rest of the way, landing flat on your face and stomach. From upstairs, there are more footsteps. You get to your feet and run for the cellar door.

"Hannah!" you call. The cellar door is closed. You yank hard, but it doesn't budge. "Hannah!" you call again.

There's no answer. There are only more footsteps, coming from the top of the stairs. Then a foot lands heavy on the top step.

You dash for the front door but instead of hanging open, it's closed, and no amount of pushing on it opens it. It's like it's locked . . . from the outside. You dash toward the back of the house. There has to be a back-door. And sure enough, you come to a door. More footsteps. Whoever it is, they are definitely coming down.

"Hannah!" you shout once more. "James!"

No answer. You shove on the back door. It opens and you are outside. The cool fresh night air greets you. You call for Hannah and James once more. And when you turn to look back inside, a shadow fills the hallway. It stands next to the cellar door, not moving.

You run. You hate leaving Hannah behind, but maybe she already ran and left you behind. She's probably back at camp, naked next to James in a sleeping bag. You circling around the cabin and back down the dirt driveway, and then you push your way through the woods.

You run way longer than you remember coming. You call out for your friends. But you can't find them and you can't find the campsite. The woods are dark and deep, and you have to admit that you're lost.

You pull your broken cell phone out, but now, with the cracked screen, it won't even turn on. Shit. And then, from back the way you came, you hear a low voice call, "Helloooooooo."

You take off, pushing through the trees. You run in a single direction. It has to lead somewhere. And sure enough, your efforts are rewarded. You come to a road paved with gravel instead of dirt. It's got to lead to civilization.

You walk for fifteen minutes in complete silence. You try to keep it together. And then, from behind you, you hear the sound of an engine.

It's a car. Your friends! You spin around just as the car comes to a stop next to you.

It's definitely not your friends, and it's not your rental van. Instead it's a man and a woman wearing matching plaid shirts. They don't look like serial killers. Just hillbillies.

"You need a ride, sweetie?" the woman asks.

Normally you would never take a ride from a stranger, but these are not normal times.

If you take a ride from the couple, turn to page 94.

No way are you getting in the car with these people. Turn to page 82.

S ure, you could look for another exit, but what if there isn't one? The best bet it to try to break down the door. And given that this is a creepy basement with all sorts of killing implements, there has to be something around that can help.

From deep in the basement, you both hear a laugh.

"What is that?" Hannah asks between her sobs.

"A psycho killer?" you say. Not that you think it will help. What will help is if she stops crying. You scour the basement, throwing aside knives and hammers and screwdrivers. And finally you find an ax. You grab it and rush up the stairs. And then you start chopping away at the wood of the door.

It's a lot harder to chop through a door than you would have thought. You swing and put more force behind it. There's a chuckling from the dark, and then the sound of wood scraping on wood.

"Hurry!" Hannah shouts. "Someone is coming."

You want to point out that if she helped, it might be better. But she's useless. It's up to you. You keep chopping. The footsteps turn into a shadow, and it's getting closer. And closer. And just when you think it's never going to work, you swing the ax, and it cuts clean through.

Wood splinters everywhere, and you're able to reach outside and undo the lock.

"Come on!" you shout to Hannah, and then you're through the door.

Hannah runs up the steps. The shadow is so close. She's almost to the top. Then she trips. And falls. And the shadow swallows her.

You have about two seconds of indecision, and then you are out the front door of the cabin and dashing back for the campground. Claire is there, mumbling something about Joey getting killed by some psycho, and there is no sign of James. But you and Claire grab the keys to the van, and you are out of there.

Later, when you tell the police what happened, they don't believe you. And when they go back to check the cabin, there is nothing creepy there. No blood stains. No knifes and pliers. No sign of Hannah. But you know what you saw.

At least you are alive.

THE END

Okay, this whole thing was a bad idea. Coming into a dark cave, following some crying sound that may or may not be real. And that's when you remember. What if it's not real? What if this is a ghost? Claire had told that story about the little girl who went missing? What had she said? That her parents brought her into the woods and left her? And that when they'd gone back to try to find her, they went missing and were never found. Like some kind of twisted Hansel and Gretel. What if the little girl went into this cave to try and find a safe place to stay and never came out? What if, when her parents came looking for you, she killed them as revenge?

Okay, ghosts aren't real, and that's just ridiculous. Your mind is coming up with nonsense. Still, the crying has stopped, and there is no sign of anyone in this cave. It's time to get back to your friends and enjoy the camping trip that you came here for.

You turn, take a step, and fall into a deep pit. You twist an ankle and hit your head on a rock, but otherwise, you're okay. Sadly, your cell phone isn't. It's cracked and there is no chance the flashlight will turn on. Shit. This is not a good situation. Pitch black at the bottom of a pit in a cave.

Then they crying starts again. It's coming from right here, in this pit. And a ghostly glow appears. Within the glow, is a little girl. She's dressed in torn clothes that look like they might have been in style back in the early 1900s. Her face is scratched and her hair is straggly. She's crying. But then her eyes land on you, and she smiles.

"You can take my place," she says. And then she vaporizes and the crying stops.

You shout for your friends. They don't come. You shout some more. But nobody can hear you and nobody is coming. You're hungry and thirsty and scared, and soon you're crying. You know you're going to die here, which makes you cry even more. And you can't help but notice how similar the sound of your crying is to that of the little girl.

THE END

You've seen enough people die in horror movies that you know it never works out like people think it will. If you wait for these rednecks to come set you free, you're as good as dead. So instead, you clench your teeth together, grab hold of either side of the bear trap, and pull. Pain courses through your body. You scream. You can't help it. You pull harder.

"Look what it's trying to do," you hear one of the rednecks say. They're getting closer.

You pull more. You scream more. And then, as adrenaline pumps through your body, you find strength you never knew you had. The pain is blissful as the bear trap pulls free and releases.

Blood is everywhere. Your foot feels like it's been cut off. But you are free!

You stand, but the second you try to put weight on that leg, you fall.

"Get it!" one of the rednecks shouts.

Hell no. You take off running, pushing the pain out of your mind. There's time to suffer later. For now, the only objective you have is to get free.

You try to find camp, but you're all turned around. You don't know where your friends are. You don't know where the camp is. All you know is you have to put distance between you and the bear trap-hunting rednecks.

Time moves in a blur as you stumble through the woods. And when you finally break free of the trees, the sun is just showing its face above the horizon. With the light, you find a main road, and soon reach a small town.

You tell the police what happened, but they don't believe you at first. They tell you the serial killers known as the Twisted Twins haven't shown their faces in years. But you beg them to go back and look for your friends. They do, and they find them—at least parts of them. They have large swathes of skin missing. Their fingernails are gone. Their tongues are cut out. And their eyes . . . Well, you'll never be able to get the image of that out of your mind. You are the only one who made it out alive.

The police look everywhere for the redneck brothers—the Twisted Twins—with no success. Wherever they are, they're still out there. Waiting for you. And you know you will never go camping again.

THE END

You try to send mental thoughts to Joey, letting him know to hold on. That you're coming. Then you look around. There are a couple of other tunnels and some kind of storage area. And bingo! In the storage area are some of the robes, both red and black.

Wait. Which color should you pick? They've got to mean different things. You spend way too long trying to decide. This isn't some fashion statement. Your friend is about to get sacrificed and killed, and here, you're trying to decide which color looks better on you?

Black. It's way more slimming and . . .

Oh my god, what are you thinking? Your friend is dying! You grab the black robe and throw it on over your clothes. Wait. What if these people don't wear anything under their robes? You roll your pant legs up just to cover your bases.

As you hurry back to the main chamber, the chanting gets louder. You catch weird words here and there. *Diaboli. Satan. Lucifer.*

Oh crap. You've found the satanic cult. The same one Joey's parents had warned him about, and now here he is about to get sacrificed by them.

You have zero clue what you are doing, but you edge your way into the room, keeping the hood on your robe well over your face. You mumble words and move around like they are, swaying. You scoot closer and closer to Joey. He has cuts everywhere. On his arms. His face. There's even a pentagram carved into his stomach. There is blood everywhere. You almost throw up. This is a horrible idea and you need to get out of here.

The chanting gets louder and louder. You blend in, more humming than saying words. And then, everyone goes silent . . .

. . . except you.

You aren't expecting them to stop chanting. All eyes turn to you as you clasp a hand over your mouth. Way too late.

Then they are on you. They strip off your robe and your clothes and strap you on the stone altar next to Joey.

"What are you doing?" he asks.

"Saving you," you start to say, but that's when you feel the first cut of the dagger. You scream, and you wonder if Claire or James or Hannah will come looking for you two. But even if they did, by then, you know it would be too late.

THE END

"Yoo hoo!" the man calls down.

You don't move. You try not to breathe. It's dark for you. It's dark for him.

A piece of dirt is tickling you under your nose, and you're about to sneeze, but you are a champion. You hold it in. You don't make a sound. Your very life depends on how quiet and still you can be.

Then the guy starts laughing. "One more for the cemetery," he says. And then he raises the thing he's holding. It's a shovel.

You start scrambling just as the first scoop of fresh soil comes down on top of you, hitting you on top of the head, getting in your eyes. You brush it off as another shovelful falls. Then another.

"Stop!" you try to shout, but when you open your mouth, you get a mouthful of dirt. This guy is like some kind of shoveling maniac. Like he does this for a living.

Wait. Shit. The Ghostly Gravedigger. Destined to bury any who cross his path. Wasn't that the urban legend that Hannah told? Oh shit, you need to get out of here.

You scrape your fingers on the sides of the grave, but the dirt is heavy and thick and coming fast. It's building up around your legs. You try to pull a foot free, but it's stuck. The next clump of dirt knocks you over.

You don't get back up. And as the last shovelful of soil covers your eyes, blocking all light, you lie there thinking how you wished you'd stayed to set up the campsite instead.

THE END

There are a few truths in life. One: if you don't feed your pet fish, they will die. Two: open beer is never good the next morning after a party. And three: scarecrows are not alive.

"Not alive," you say, and then you start climbing. One hand after another. One foot, then the next. You make your way to the top. This pole is way higher than you thought. You break free from the corn and can finally see over. But from this low, you still can't see the way out. So, you climb higher. Five more feet. You can kind of see the edges of the cornfield, but everything looks the same. There is forest everywhere. A little higher. Then you can't put it off. You climb right up next to the scarecrow.

"Not alive," you say again.

Now you are at the very top. You can see everything from here. The forest that goes on forever, but there are some landmarks you can follow. The mountains, still visible in the moonlight. A black curving line that may be the main road. And smoke curling up from between the trees. That's it. That has to be the campsite. Whew. Relief flows through you. Claire has probably already found her way back there and is waiting for you.

You lower yourself one rung. Or at least you try to, but your shirt catches on something. You twist around and come face to face with the scarecrow.

"Alive," he says. His sewn-up mouth pulls open with the words. His eyes try to suck you in.

"Oh shit!" you shout, and you try to reach behind and free yourself. Your shirt is hooked on a nail.

Then the stitching of his mouth unravels and the thread flows toward you, like it has a mind of its own. It digs into your lips, and you scream. You keep screaming until the scarecrow reaches up and pulls the thread tight. The straw comes next, flying out of him, into you. Then it's the clothes. One thing at a time and you are slowly turning into him. And he . . . he's turning into you. The black splotches and burlap bag are gone, now replaced with your smooth skin. Then one eye at a time, he finishes the job.

With your soulless eyes you watch as he climbs down. You're unable to say a word. Unable to move. All you can do is watch as he sets off, through the corn, back in the direction of the campsite. Will your friends know it's not you? Will he hurt them?

You'll never know. Because you vow that you will never do to anyone else what's been done to you. But as day after day and week after week passes, your view on this changes. And so you wait for some unsuspecting victim to come your way and give you a chance at freedom.

THE END

If you give up on the maze now, that's going to be a horrible mistake. You logic it out. If you make a bunch of left turns and you come back to this same sign, then you'll know you're trapped in a loop and you'll push your way out. But until then, you have to stay the course.

You have no cell phone signal, but your phone still has charge, so you take a picture of the creepy death symbol. Then you head left. And left. And left. You try to ignore the giggling, like a child playing a game. You try to tell yourself it's all in your mind, but you're not stupid. Someone is in this corn maze with you, and they're totally fucking with you.

You take a final left turn, follow the path, and you're dumped into a clearing. There it is. The way out! Wait, not quite a clearing. On all four sides of you are walls of corn. Wait, this isn't the way out. It's the center of the corn maze.

You've got to go back the way you came. You turn back around, just in time to see a little red-headed kid wearing overalls and holding a scythe. He giggles and points at you. You open your mouth to speak. But before a word can leave your mouth, he lifts the scythe and swings it for your head.

THE END

You can't stop yourself. "Hello?" you say one more time.

There is no response. The chair just keeps rocking and rocking. You step into the room, tiptoeing. Maybe they can't hear you. Maybe they're deaf. Maybe . . .

Okay, you can't think of any plausible explanation. You move closer. You can't see who is there. But there has to be someone. The chair is not rocking itself. You take one more step, and the floorboard creaks under your foot. Shit.

The rocking chair stops.

You're only a few steps away. So, you take the last few steps and turn so you can see. In the rocking chair is a woman. She's got stringy gray hair. Her face is wrinkled and gaunt. She's wearing a hospital gown. She looks up at you and smiles with a toothless smile.

"I found my babies," she says.

Her babies?

"Did you know I had twins?" she says.

Your eyes drift to her arms. To what she is holding there. Cradled in her right arm, James's lifeless eyes stare back at you. In her left arm, Hannah looks up at you. Blood seeps from their necks, covering the hospital gown.

"I've been looking for them everywhere," she says. "I found them. And I'm never going to let them go."

You step back and you scream. And then you turn and run. Out of the bedroom. Down the stairs. Out the front door. And back to the campsite. You grab James's keys from where he threw them earlier, and you jump in the car. You have no idea where Joey and Claire are, but as long as they are far away from the cabin, they'll be fine. Then you drive, back down the dirt road, until you find a police station.

You tell them what happened, and they send some squad cars out. They find Joey and Claire who were smoking inside one of the tents. Then they find the cabin. The woman is still there, rocking.

The police fill you in on the story. A patient escaped from a local insane asylum. A woman. A mother. She'd given birth to twins fifty years ago, but they'd both died, and she'd never gotten over it. She'd always been looking for her lost babies.

You mourn when you think of James and Hannah, but you're also very happy that she didn't have triplets.

THE END

That cellar door is made of solid wood. Trying to break it down will take forever. And the longer you spend in this cellar, the less time you want to be here. You need to get out of here now. You shine your cell phone light around again, looking for an alternate exit. Each time the light lands on a splatter of blood, you nearly lose it, but with Hannah blubbering next to you, you need to keep it together.

"This way," you say, shining the light off to the right. There's a wooden bookshelf filled with tools, and behind it, there is an opening.

"You sure?" Hannah asks, wiping her eyes.

"I'm sure."

Actually, you're not sure about anything. From the shelves, you grab a hammer . . . just in case. You don't want to think about what "just in case" might mean, but it can't hurt to be prepared.

The opening ahead of you is covered in cobwebs. You brush them aside and step through. Spiders skitter on the walls. One falls on Hannah, and she screams—really loud.

"Shhh . . . ," you say. If there is anyone down here—besides James—then you don't want them to hear you.

As you walk along in the dark, the floor and walls change. Before, the floor was hard-packed dirt and the walls were made of wood planks, but here the floor and walls seem to be made of rocks. It's like this place was carved out of solid stone.

"Where are we going?" Hannah asks.

You shine the light around. There's only one way to go. "This way."

She nods like you've given her the answer to the meaning of life.

The path goes on for maybe thirty feet and then it opens up into a small room. There are shelves with glass jars lining all the walls. A root cellar! This is great news! Most root cellars have a direct exit to the outside. You shine the light around, and it reflects off one of the jars.

What the . . . ?

You step closer and hold the light so you can see inside the jar. There aren't carrots or beets stored inside. There are eyeballs. At least ten eyeballs. The jar next to it has the tips of fingers—including the fingernails— and the jar next to that has teeth.

Hannah accidentally sees that one and lets out a shriek that rattles your eardrums.

Holy shit, you need to get out of here. You shine the light up, and there are the doors to the outside.

"Come on, Hannah," you say, but she shrieks again.

Then, from out of the dark, a hand clamps over her mouth. Her scream is stopped immediately. Then the hand pulls her backward, into the darkness.

"Hannah!" you shout, and you start to run after her. But your head slams into something—or something slams into your head—and you black out.

You wake to find yourself strapped to a metal chair, bound at the wrists and ankles. The walls around you are wooden planks, but it's not the cellar. You turn your head, and there in the chair next to you is Hannah. Except pieces of her are missing. And you're pretty sure she's not alive. And in another chair is James . . . you think. It's hard to even recognize him. Why you're still alive, you have no idea. But you'd like to keep it that way.

If you scream for help and then try to attack whatever psycho did this when he comes into the room, turn to page 84.

If you stay quiet and try to find a way out of this, turn to page 105.

The chirping stops. Then it starts again. It reminds you of cicadas, except the entire cave would have to be packed with cicadas for them to make a sound this loud. You take a step toward it. It changes in cadence. Louder. Shifting. The chirping fills your ears.

You take a few more steps, and your foot gets stuck. You pull it out of some weird patch of mucus, in a puddle. There's another puddle of it. Then another. You try to avoid it, but you brush up against a wall, and the mucus is there, too. That's what all the dripping earlier was. It's not water. It's this sticky, gooey stuff.

By now, the chirping is so loud it makes you want to cover your ears. Could whatever insect is making this sound have made the crying sound earlier? An insect being able to make a sound like that doesn't seem out of the realm of possibilities. Then you step forward into a chamber. The chirping is loudest here, but there are no insects that you see. What you do see will haunt your forever though. Up against the walls are four sacks that look like they're made from a semi-clear membrane. They're filled with mucus, and inside each is one of your friends. Hannah. James. Claire. Joey.

Oh god, this is horrible. You hurry to the one with Joey inside, and using your fingernails, you rake at the membrane. It jumps, and Joey's eyes open wide. He's still alive. But his mouth opens, and mucus begins to pool inside, and as you watch, he gags and chokes. You try and try to break free, to get him out, but it's no use. And then Joey is dead.

The chirping is deafening now, and you hear skittering. You whip around . . . and come face to face with a cicada the size of a golden doodle. Five others flank it. Then the bug jabs something in your mouth. You know it's going to cover you in this mucus in two hot seconds, and that you're going to die, just like your friends. The mucus slithers down your throat, nearly gagging you.

Then, before you can process what is happening, the chirping stops, and the bugs all skitter away, disappearing into the shadows. You don't breathe for a solid minute. You wait. But the bugs are not coming back. You check each of your friends, but none of them are moving. There is no saving them, but you can still save yourself.

You backtrack out of the cave, back to the campsite, and back to the world.

Turn to page 112.

You pry at the bear trap once more and almost pass out from the pain. No way are you going to be able to get it off on your own. These rednecks can't be all that smart, anyway. Literally, who lives out in the woods hunting down people with a bear trap?

Wait. Then you remember. The serial killers known as the Twisted Twins. This was how they operated. They caught campers unaware, and then they peel off their skin and make lampshades from them. Oh, this is not good. You try one more time to get the bear trap off, but it's not budging.

You hear them coming, talking back and forth the whole time.

"This one's gonna be good eating," one says.

Eating! What about the skin peeling thing? Not that either is a good choice.

"We should free it and let it run," says the other. "Toughen up its meat a little."

"How 'bout those other two we caught. You hear them squeal?" one says.

The other two they caught? That could be James and Hannah. Or Joey and Claire.

Oh god, what has happened to your friends?

Then the twins are right there, standing over you.

"Hey, little pig. You git yerself stuck?" one of the rednecks says.

You don't answer. Terror pulsates through you. You are going to die . . . unless you can get away from them. Tears spill out of your eyes. Your whole body is shaking.

"I'll unstick ya," the redneck says. And he takes each side of the bear trap in a meaty hand and yanks it open. Then he lets it slam shut again.

You let out a blood-curdling scream. It would be better if they just killed you now.

"Don't play with yer food," the other redneck says. And he takes a key from a chain hanging from his side and unlocks the bear trap.

Pain and relief mingle inside you. But there's no time to enjoy these feeling. While he's still leaning down over you, you take the tent stake that is still clenched in your hand, and you jam it in the side of his head.

His eyes go wide. His mouth drops open. Then he topples over and falls to the ground.

One down.

The brother still standing looks to the ground. Then looks to you. His face is covered with disbelief. This is your chance to run. But if you leave this brother alive, he could track you down.

If you run like hell, turn to page 86.

If you kill the other brother, turn to page 96.

Yeah, sure, putting on a robe and saving Joey all by yourself might make you a hero, but if you fail . . . Well, it's no good being a hero if you're dead.

"I'll come back for you, man," you whisper too low for any of the people wearing robes to hear.

Almost like he hears you, Joey screams again. Oh wait, maybe that's because they just pulled his toenail out. Ick.

You step backward, then again. And down the small hall you go until you come to the bottom of the stairs . . . or at least where the bottom of the stairs should be. A smooth flat panel covers the entryway. You prod your fingers around, looking for some kind of lever or pulley, (yes, the irony that if you'd saved Joey and he were here next to you, he could probably build one does not escape you) but there is nothing to be found. Sweat beads up on your forehead. Is the chanting getting louder or is that your imagination.

Joey screams again. You have to get out of here and find Claire and the others. Then you can all come down here and kick some crazy cult member ass. You turn left, then right. There, to the right is a tunnel. There must be a way out that way. You start down it, praying you don't run into any wayward cult members. Five steps. Ten steps. Twenty steps away. You finally start to breathe. Then Joey screams again, but this time it's long and drawn out and fizzles more than stops. Almost like he's—

No, you can't finish that thought. Joey can't be dead.

Except you have a really bad feeling that he is.

Dead.

Shit.

You need to get out of here.

You stumble down the corridor, getting as far away from this cult as possible. There's some kind of light ahead. If you can just reach that, you'll be safe. But you trip, and make a god awful sound that everyone in this underground cavern must've heard.

"Is someone there?" a voice calls out. "Please, help us."

"Help, please," another voice croaks.

"Save me!" a third voice begs in a hoarse whisper.

Still on the ground, you turn your head to the left. You can barely make out the outline of iron bars. It's some kind of dungeon. Beyond it are at least ten people, naked and afraid.

You push yourself up to your knees and pull on the grate. It's locked . . . of course. Because if it wasn't locked, why would these people be stuck behind it?

"Help us!" one of the people says. "Open the gate."

"It's locked," you say, even though they already know this.

"There's a key," someone manages to garble out. From how hoarse their voices are, it sounds like they haven't had water in days.

"Where?" you ask, looking around. Hopefully there's a hook on the wall with the key hanging on it.

One of them points back the way you came. He's dirty and hairy and looks like he hasn't showered in a year. "That way. Near the stairs."

Um, yeah, that's a big no. No way are you going back toward the crazy cult that just killed your friend.

"I didn't see a key," you say, making a paltry attempt to pull the gate open once more.

"It's there," the dirty, hairy guy says. "I swear."

Maybe there's a key. Maybe there's not. But going back to look for it is a sure death sentence. Except if there is a chance you can free these people, then you really should try.

If you go back for the key and help them escape, turn to page 98.

If you leave them locked away and look for the exit, turn to page 88.

"Anyone down there?" the guy calls.

There's something in the tone of his voice that makes you certain he can see you. You can feel his eyes fixed on you, even though you can't see his face. If you stay here, he's probably going to bury you alive.

Thank god for that rock climbing elective you took back in college. You stand up, claw your fingers into the soft soil walls, and begin climbing.

"Look who's coming to play," the guy says, and then he chortles.

Hell yeah you're coming to play. And this mother fucker better watch out.

As you're nearing the top, he lifts whatever he's holding. It's a shovel. He swings it, and you barely duck out of the way. And then you're out of the grave. You took about a month of kung fu back sophomore year in college, and you barely got past short kata number four. Still, it's all you have.

You punch him with kung fu short kata number one. He's not expecting that and he doubles over. You move on to short kata number two. Then three. And when you get to short kata number four (the last one you know), you sweep his legs out from under him and push him into the grave. Then you turn and you run like the very devil is chasing you. You clear the cemetery. You're back in the trees. You run and run, and you find the clearing where you, Joey, and Claire were looking for firewood. There's some kind of contraption you're sure Joey built, but there's no sign of either of them.

"They're back at the campsite," you tell yourself, and you push on, down the path that will lead you there.

Sweet relief washes over you when you step into the campsite. Five tents are up. There's wood in the fire-pit. But . . . there is no sign of any of your friends. The van is still there, right where James left it. They must be off looking for . . . well, you aren't sure what. But something. So, you grab a beer from the cooler and sink down into one of the camp chairs.

You take a long sip of the beer, drinking well over half of it, and then you rest your hand on the arm rest. Which is wet. And sticky. And . . .

You lift your hand and look at it. It's covered in blood.

You bolt to your feet and take a better look around. There is blood everywhere. On the tents. The chairs. A large piece of firewood is off to the side of the firepit and looks like it has blood and hair covering one end. Long blond hair, just like Hannah has.

You get a horrible feeling in the pit of your stomach that your friends are all dead. And you know you'll be dead too unless you get the hell out of here. But what if they're still alive? Maybe you should look for them.

If you get in the van and drive away, turn to page 102.

If you look for your friends, turn to page 90.

That scarecrow moved. You know it. Whether it's on some pivot thing or whether it's alive and ready to eat you, you don't care. You are not climbing this pole. Instead, you take off running.

You're sure you run a straight line, but ten minutes later, and you're right back at the scarecrow. You look up. Yep. It's looking back the other way. You run again, and once again, you're back at the scarecrow. It's turned once more. Again, you run, and again it's the same freaking thing. You can't seem to shake this fucker.

Then, as you're watching, it cocks its head. It stretches its arms. Bits of straw fall, landing in your hair. And it begins to climb down. You have to get out of here. Have to get back to safety. Because you know if this thing catches you, you will die.

And then, almost like you're channeling your high school Astronomy teacher, you spot a star in the sky. The North Star. It used to guide sailors. It's gonna guide you the hell out of here.

You run. And this time, you keep checking the North Star. Making sure you're heading in the correct direction. Keeping it consistently aligned to you.

Corn rustles behind you. It's got to be the scarecrow. But you can't look back. You plow ahead, through the corn, until after what feels like eternity, you break free. But you don't stop there. You run back into the woods, through the trees and the clearing, until you wind up back at the campsite.

There, sitting around a blazing fire, are James, Hannah, Claire, and Joey. Roasting marshmallows. Drinking beer. Laughing about god knows what. But the laughter stops when the scarecrow breaks into the campsite.

"The fuck is that?" James asks, jumping to his feet, stumbling backward.

For some weird reason, you want to prove just how brave you are. So, you dive at the scarecrow, grabbing it around the waist. It's not expecting that. And then, in one fluid movement, you toss the thing right into the firepit. All the straw and the raggedy clothes immediately catch. And as you watch it burn, you grab a beer from the cooler, open it, and take a long sip.

"That, my friends, is a dead scarecrow," you say. "Now let's get this party started."

THE END

Forget the rules of a maze. You're turned right enough times that you should have long ago found your way out of there. This is no maze. This is some psycho's idea of fun, and you want no part of it.

You grab stalks of corn in either hand and spread them, pushing your way through. You tunnel through the corn. You're making great progress (or so you tell yourself). And then you come into an opening. One of the paths. That's okay. You do it again, grabbing the corn and shoving it to the side. You tunnel once again. Again, you wind up in the maze. You think back to how big the "biggest" corn maze was when you were a child. It couldn't have covered a very large area. So, you keep at it. And keep at it. And finally, your hard work pays off. You come to the edge of the cornfield.

You celebrate by taking out your cell phone for a selfie with that stupid cornfield behind you. Screw that place. You smile. Take the picture. Then you turn and take another one of the vast wide open that is your path to sweet freedom.

You smile. The flash goes off. But then you notice something strange in the picture. Something behind you. You turn slowly, and there ahead of you are five poles stuck into the soil. Atop four of the poles are the heads of your four friends. Joey. Hannah. Claire. James. They're all there, and they're all dead.

You start running, and immediately trip over a rope that's been tied across the path. You land flat on your face. And when you turn over to get up. A shape looms over you. It's a kid holding a scythe. He smiles at you and says, "You broke the rules of the maze."

Then the scythe comes down and lops off your head.

THE END

Who cares if they seem nice and helpful? That's just what they want you to think to lull you into a false sense of security. But you don't want them to think you don't trust them.

"Oh, no, I'm fine," you say. "My friends are just up ahead." You hope that part is true.

"Are ya sure?" the man asks.

"I'm sure," you say, and then, because your heart is still pounding, you turn and continue walking down the road. You don't look at the car. You don't look back. But you hear the car creeping along behind you.

You consider ducking into the woods again, but you don't want to get lost. Still the car keeps following you. You walk as quickly as you can. Then you run. The car speeds up, too. You have no choice. If you don't get off this road, they're going to run you down.

You try to juke them out by dashing left and then dashing back to the right. And then you shove your way between two huge trees.

You run for about thirty seconds and then you stop, trying to catch your breath. You don't move. You can still see the car headlights from here. Then it blows its horn once and drives off.

Whew.

Now to find your friends.

You hurry back to the road since the car is long gone. But just as you come out of the trees, a shape materializes in front of you. It's bulky and looming and holding a baseball bat. You try to turn and run, but there is no time. And the last thing you remember is the baseball bat coming right at your head.

THE END

You work out the plan in your head. The only way to live through this is by being proactive. You'll scream to draw the psycho in here. Then, you'll grab whatever he's holding and stab him with it instead. Perfect!

You start screaming, so loud it makes your head hurt. You half expect Hannah and James to wake up at the sound, but, yeah, one glance at them and you know that's never going to happen. There is no saving them. But there is saving yourself. You scream and scream, but nobody comes. But you don't give up. You scream some more, and finally you hear footsteps above you, maybe coming from the creepy cabin. It's working. You keep screaming!

Off in the distance, you hear a door open—the cellar door you hope—and then footsteps begin coming down the stairs.

"Help me! Let me out!" you scream. This screaming stuff is hard work. You're not sure how Hannah managed it. Just when you think you can't scream any more, the door to the room you're in opens.

In walks a burly man in a pair of denim overalls and a red undershirt.

"Shut your damn mouth!" he says.

And you keep on screaming.

Then he comes at you, and he's holding something. This is your moment. Except the man arm bars you and raises his other hand.

"Then I'll shut you up!" he says. You realize he's holding a pair of tongs, and they're coming right for your face.

You try to shut your mouth, but he's fast and crafty and he grabs your tongue. Oh shit. He reaches with his other hand to his waist and grabs a hunting knife. Then in one solid motion, he cuts off your tongue.

You're sobbing and screaming and it hurts like a motherfucker.

"Now that was fun, wasn't it?" he says. He takes your now cut off tongue and places it in a jar, then seals the lid. On the table where he sets it are at least fifteen more jars. Then he turns back to you with the tongs in one hand and the knife in the other, and he smiles. "What's next?"

THE END

Sure, you got lucky and killed one brother, but you can't waste time trying to kill the other. The best thing to do is run like hell, and see if you can find your friends. At the thought of them, you get a giant lump in your throat. Don't let them be dead. But you'll worry about that later.

With your good leg, you swipe out and sweep the redneck off his feet. He falls flat on his butt, landing next to his dead brother. He starts screaming and hugging on his brother, and this is your chance.

You stand as best you can, and limping, you take off through the woods. You have to get back to the campsite. You have to get away. The trees are dense, but you finally reach a clearing in the trees. There's something hanging up ahead, but you can't make it out in the dark. You slow down, step closer. And then, with your next step, a rope tightens around your ankle.

You're pulled up into the air as you hear a weight slam to the ground. And then you're upside down, dangling by one ankle. Shit.

As you twist and swing, you turn so you can get a good look at whatever you saw earlier. And there, dangling from a nearby tree, is Joey. His throat has been cut, and a pool of dark blood covers the ground under him.

That's when you hear the leaves crunching in the woods. Footsteps come closer to you. You struggle and try to free yourself, but then the redneck brother is in front of you. He smiles with a toothless grin, and he says, "Looks like you got yerself stuck."

Then he lifts a giant hunting knife to your neck and laughs.

THE END

You want to be a nice person. You really do. And saving these people would be really nice. But you know what else would be nice? Not getting captured and killed by a psychotic satanic cult. Yeah, that would be way nicer than taking the hero route.

You make yourself a deal. When you get out of here, you'll contact the police. You'll tell them about these people. Sure, maybe one or two will get sacrificed before the police get here, but going by straight statistics, that only at most 20%. Which means that you'll be able to save maybe 80% of them and save yourself. The math makes sense. You're glad you listened in math class. Turns out math is useful in the real world.

"Are you listening?" the hairy guy says.

You shake your head, snapping yourself out of the battle to do what's right. "Oh, yeah, sorry. I was just calculating—"

"Just get the key!" one of them screams.

Far off, the chanting stops. The satanic cult has heard. That's your cue to get the hell outta here.

"Sorry, I can't help," you say. "I'll send the police."

Then you take off running, continuing on your way. The prisoners are screaming and yelling, and you hear footsteps pounding behind you. You run way faster than you ever did back in elementary school for the 50 yard dash. This is life or death.

One of the people screams, "Someone was here! They went that way!"

They are seriously ratting you out to the cult members? Forget sending the police. They can sort this one out on their own. And then you keep running.

You count your steps. You stumble. And then, when you're sure they're just behind you, you see a light. It glows like the moon (or maybe the cemetery, but anything is better than this.) And you give it your all, bursting out into the open. But you don't stop there. You run and run, through trees and brush with mountains on your side. You don't dare turn around until the only footsteps you can hear are your own. Only then, next to a small creek, do you dare to stop.

Behind you, there is no sign of any satanic cult members. Except unless they were wearing the black and red robes, how would you know if they were in the cult or not? Shit, for all you know, the police could be members of the cult. Someone has to be. And the truth sinks in on you. You can never tell anyone what happened back there, even though that means no one will ever know what happened to Joey. You can never mention the cult. Because if you do, they'll come after you. They'll grab you and put you in that dungeon, waiting to sacrifice you. It sucks, but it's reality. And all you can do is hope that the cult never finds you.

THE END

These four were your very best friends, and even though it sure as hell looks like they all got bludgeoned to death, if that's the case, then where are the bodies? You have to at least look for them.

You finish your beer (why waste a good beer?) and then, holding the neck, you crack the glass bottle on the bricks of the firepit. Now you have a weapon. You check your cell phone again, but there's still no signal. It's up to you to save your friends.

You channel your inner scout and look to the ground for tracks. There are splatters of blood against that tree trunk. Pieces of hair tangled in that bush. It looks like something got dragged between these two trees. Slowly, one clue at a time, you follow a trail. And with each step forward, your confidence grows. Also, it makes you sure your friends are still alive. After all, why drag dead bodies through a forest? The trees thicken. You almost lose the trail. Then you see a torn piece of the blue hoodie James was wearing. In some weird way, you're really thankful you were trapped at the bottom of an empty grave. Otherwise, whatever happened to your friends would have also happened to you.

You trek through the woods for a solid fifteen minutes, doubling back every so often to make sure you haven't lost the trail. And then you turn a corner and come into a clearing.

They're hanging by chains from thick tree branches. As Claire's body slowly turns, you see a giant meat hook embedded in her back. Hannah, also hanging by a meat hook, has half her head bashed in. James is shirtless, and his chest and back are covered in blood. And Joey . . .

Wait, Joey's moaning. He's still alive!

You dash over to him, drop the empty beer bottle, and you almost pull him down. But with the meat hook, that may not be the best idea.

"I'm here, man," you say, and you try to lift him off the hook.

He shrieks, a piercing noise that sounds through the night air.

"What happened?" you ask him.

All he manages is a moan in response, and then he dies.

That's when you notice the fifth chain and meat hook hanging there, empty . . . waiting for you.

Not if you can help it.

You run, leaving your dead friends behind. All the fun you thought this camping trip would be . . . All the good times . . . Now your friends are dead, and you're the only one left alive. You keep turning back, because you're sure someone is following you, but you don't see anyone or anything. And then, when you're pretty sure you've run for miles, you break free onto the road.

You pull out your cell phone. Five bars. Civilization! You dial 911, and as the operator answers, you turn back to the woods one last time. From the trees, a man covered in blood stands watching, holding a baseball bat. He gives you a smile and waves, as if to say "see you soon," and then he turns and walks away.

THE END

You have to get away from whoever was in the cabin, because if they find you, you are a goner for sure. And this is probably just some sweet married couple out for an evening drive. Okay, that's probably not the case, but what choice do you have?

"Thank you," you say. "Can you take me to a phone?" If you can get to a phone, you can call the police. They can come check out the cabin and help you get back to the campsite. Shit, your friends are all probably sitting around right now, drinking beers, telling ghost stories. And you're stuck on some back road with two redneck lovebirds.

"Git on in," the woman says.

You open the back door and climb in, and they take off down the dark, empty road. It's weird, because now that you're in the car, neither of them speaks. They look straight ahead. They don't smile.

"Do you guys live around here?" you ask.

No answer.

"Do you know where the campsite is?"

No answer.

"Have you seen my friends?"

No answer.

With each question, you realize what a very bad idea this whole thing was. And after about ten minutes, you say, "You know, I think I'll walk from here. Can you stop and let me out?"

No answer.

"Stop!"

This time you get a response. The man and the woman look at each other and smile.

Shit. You pull on the door handle, but the door doesn't open. You look for the lock, but it's been removed. Shit. Shit. Shit.

"Let me out!" you shout.

The woman finally turns around to look at you. "Someone needs to shut ya up," she says. "Has anyone ever told ya that ya talk too much?"

Then she reaches back with a damp cloth. You struggle with her, trying to keep it away, but she's wiry and strong, and she shoves it over your mouth and nose. You try not to breathe in, but it's no use. Then the world goes black.

Turn to page 108.

ure, this guy seems upset now, but within minutes, he'll be after you, hot on your trail. And with your foot hanging on by barely a tendon, it's not like you'll be able to run far away from him.

You try to pull the tent spike out of the head of his brother, but the thing is wedged in there good. Maybe caught on the space where his brain should be?

"Yer gonna die," the redneck says, and he wipes his hands on his overalls, where you notice a large hunting knife. He places a hand on it. So maybe you can't wrestle it from him, but if he has one . . .

You look to the dead brother, and there at his side is a matching hunting knife. Sweet! You grab for it, scuttling along on the ground. Whatever these two brothers intended to do with their knives, you never want to find out. When it's within reach you grab the handle and pull it free. You're not a second too soon.

The other redneck lunges for you. You just have time to get the knife pointed upward. And then you use his momentum to stab him from under his chin upward.

His eyes go wide. Then he falls to the ground, landing in perfect symmetry next to his brother. And with that you finally let out a breath of relief. You are alive. Your friends . . . God, you really hope they are. And the Twisted Twins? They're dead—never to unleash their psychotic brutalities on the world again.

THE END

What kind of person would you be if you didn't help these people? Like if you were locked in a dungeon, sure to be next on the sacrificial table getting your spleen cut out, and somebody came along, you'd want them to help you. You remember Claire muttering something about karma on the drive. How if you do something nice, the universe will reward you. And if you do something shitty, then you get shit on in return.

You stop, blow out a deep breath, then turn to the hairy guy. "Where is this key?"

He grins, and he's missing three teeth. You wonder if the crazy cult members pulled them out and are wearing them as necklaces. You run your tongue over your teeth, happy all thirty-two (yes, you still have your wisdom teeth), are all safely in your mouth.

He leans close. "You go back down the corridor to where the stairs are—"

"Where the stairs were," you say. "They're closed off."

"Right, whatever," he says. "Just go there. Behind the stairway is a guard. He's got the key. Get it and bring it back."

"A guard!" you say. "You didn't say anything about a guard." Also, was there really a guard and they never saw you? Maybe this guy's wrong and there is so guard. That would be ideal.

"I'm saying something now," the guy says.

"Just hurry already before they come to get one of us," some girl says. Like the guy, she's missing a front tooth and her stringy hair looks like she's been down here for years.

"Fine, I'll be right back." You tiptoe back down the way you came. If there is a guard . . . well, what then? You took about a month of kung fu back sophomore year in college, but you barely got past short kata number four.

With each step you take, the chanting gets louder. You try not to imagine what they're doing with Joey's body, but the more you try not to think about it, the more you think about it.

"Just get the key," you mutter.

Then you come to the end of the corridor, and . . . OMG you can't believe it. The stairway is open. This is your escape. You think about it. You really do. Forget about the prisoners. You need to save yourself.

Except karma.

If you leave them, especially after saying you'd get the key and free them, then for sure you're going to die. You'll get the key, free them, and then dash up the staircase while they're still fumbling to put their shoes on.

You skirt around behind the staircase. Sure enough there is a person in a black robe sitting on a stool. You freeze. And then you hear the snoring. He's asleep! That's why you were able to sneak down here at all. And sitting on his lap, looped around his finger, is a ring with a big skeleton key on it.

You channel your inner ninja and you creep forward. His snore catches and stops, but then it picks up again. You're so close. And when you're within reach, you loop your finger through the ring and ease it out from under his finger. He shifts, clenches his fingers into a fist . . . and then relaxes. The key ring falls free.

You are back down the corridor and in front of the dungeon so fast that everyone inside thinks you failed. You gleefully hold up the key.

"Piece of cake!" you say.

"Cake . . ." the guy with the missing teeth says.

Once he's out, you don't think cake would be the best choice for his dental health.

"Open it," the girl says in her hoarse voice.

You don't want to stay down here one second longer than you need to. You put the key in the keyhole and turn it. The lock clicks and the door swings open.

Shoving against each other, they push their way out.

"You saved us," the girl says.

"Yeah, well . . ." you start, but she's already turned away.

The dirty, hairy guy waits until last. Then he puts his hand forward.

"Thank you," he says. He's got a tear in his eye. And you know in that moment that you did something good. Something really good.

"You're welcome, man," you say, and you shake his hand.

He lurches you forward, into the cell, and then he slams the door, turns the key, locking you inside.

"What are you doing?" you ask, pulling on the bars of the cell.

He smiles his gaping smile. "We can't leave the cell empty. If we do, they'll come looking for us. But if we leave you in here . . ."

Then he turns and starts to walk away.

"What about karma?" you shout.

"Fuck karma," he says. And then he's gone, leaving you to your fate.

Fuck karma indeed.

THE END

Your friends are dead. You can either accept that and live or you can die trying to find them. If they were here, they would tell you to get the hell out of Dodge.

You dash into James's tent, tearing through his sleeping bag and clothes until you find them. The keys to the minivan! You have never found something so beautiful in your life. You grab them and kiss them, and then you're back out of the tent.

Across the campsite stands a man. He watches you. He's holding a baseball bat with his left hand, casually hitting it into his right hand. A giant meat hook dangles from his belt.

"Looking for your friends?" he calls across the distance.

Your feet won't move. You need to get out of here.

"Want to join them?" He takes a step toward you. "They're dying to see you." Then he laughs at his horrible joke.

You shift your eyes to the minivan. It's only about twenty feet away. You can make it.

"Wanna try to run?" he says, as he notices you doing this.

Ain't no trying about it. You run for the minivan so fast, you might as well be flying. Then you yank the door open and clamber inside. The door slams just as he reaches it. His face presses against the glass, and his free hand reaches for the handle.

You push the lock button and want to cry at the beautiful sound of the doors locking. Then you shove the key in the ignition, turn it. It cranks to life, and you floor it.

The guy steps back and smiles.

You blast back, the way you came, through the trees, to the bridge. That's right. The rickety bridge. It held getting you here. It will hold getting you away from here. But going over the lip of the bridge, the tires thump loudly, so you slow way the hell down.

It's going to be okay. You have a car. He's on foot. You'll get across this bridge, back to the main road, and far far away.

Except maybe something happened to the engine when you went over the lip of the bridge, but the stupid thing stalls out. Shit. You know nothing about cars. If James were here, he could . . .

Right, James is dead. Claire is dead. Joey and Hannah are dead.

You put it back in Park and try starting it again. And again. It refuses to turn over. Then something lands on the hood.

It's the guy.

He lifts the baseball bat and smashes the windshield, and before you know what's happening, he drives the meat hook into your chest, under your collarbone.

The pain you feel is nothing compared to the pain when he attaches a chain to the end of the bridge and tosses you over the side. And there, as you're taking your last breaths, you see your friends hanging beside you. Best friends until the very end.

THE END

Hannah screamed, and look what happened to her. Yeah, you aren't going to be that person. Whoever has captured you is not here right now, and this is the perfect time for your escape. Maybe they're asleep. You have to take this chance.

You don't make a sound as you look around the room, not even when your eyes fall on Hannah and James. This camping trip was the worst idea ever! Not far away, but out of reach, is a table with fifteen glass jars, a few knives, and a couple pairs of tongs. They all look recently used—a thought that makes you gag. Deep breath. You've got this.

You shift a little and the chair scoots the smallest amount. Sweet! It is not bolted to the floor. You shift a little more and then a little more. The knives are still out of reach. So, you keep scooting, trying to stay as quiet as possible. But you overestimate your next scoot, and the chair bumps into the table and everything clatters to the ground. Shit.

Above you, you heard something like a chair scraping on wood. Whoever did this must have heard you. You are running out of time.

You shift again and tip the chair over. Your fingers wrap around one of the knives that have fallen, and with some clever manipulation, you twist it around and start cutting into the straps that hold you. You cut your own skin, but you can't stop. There are footsteps above you and then something that sounds like a door open-ing. You keep cutting, and the strap breaks free! But you can't stop to celebrate now. Using that hand, you cut the other three straps. You're free. But someone is coming down the stairs.

You keep the knife in hand and run for the door. Then you're back out in the root cellar.

"Come back, come back, wherever you are," a voice calls to you. It's so close.

You scamper for the doors. There's a small ladder leading up to them.

"There you are," someone says.

You turn to see a shadowed figure blocking the way you came. So, you do the only thing you can think of. You throw the knife hard. You hear it stick, and the man lets out a grunt. But you don't stick around to ad-mire your aim. You're up the ladder and shoving the doors open above you.

Sweet freedom greets you.

"Get back here!" the man shouts.

You run. And you run. Back in the direction of the campsite. There is no sign of Joey or Claire, but the keys to the van are still right where James left them in his tent. You grab them and jump in the van. Then you start it and shove it into drive . . . right as a shadowed figure slams into the driver's side window.

"I will hunt you down," the man screams. "I prom-ise."

You slam your foot on the accelerator. You don't stop. You can't stop.

It's only when you're back on the main road that you allow yourself to breathe. And you realize your right ear is throbbing. You reach up and find that you're missing your earlobe. Your mouth also hurts. A quick search with your tongue shows that a molar is gone. You shudder. Both must be back at the cabin, now preserved in a glass jar. But you consider yourself lucky. Very lucky. If you hadn't escaped, you would have ended up like Hannah and James. And you only hope that the man never makes good on his promise.

THE END

You wake up and find yourself in a dark pit. You've been stripped down to nothing but your underwear. You have no phone. No light. But there's enough light from above for you to make out your surroundings. The walls around you are made of rocky soil, hard packed. And under your bare feet, the floor is littered with bones. Human bones. You take a step and one shifts. They scrape against each other, and one cuts into the sole of your foot.

"Let me out!" you shout.

"Shut up down there," someone shouts back. A figure appears at the top of the pit, about twenty feet up. It's the woman. "Stupid pig," she says, and she throws something down at you. It's a bone, and it hits your shoulder.

"Let me out of here!" you shout again.

Then the man's shape scuttles up next to hers. "How ya doin' down there?" he calls to you.

You give him the bird.

"Well, ya just sit purdy," he says in his hillbilly accept. "When we're ready for ya, we'll git ya outta there."

Like hell you'll just sit pretty. As soon as they walk out of sight, your brain starts spinning. You try climbing, getting a handhold. But the dirt and rocks slip out from under your fingernails. You try again . . . for five minutes, and you realize it's not going to work

Then you look to your feet. Bones. Everywhere. Sharp bones that dig into the soles of your shoes. Nice!

You find two long sharp bones, each about the size of your forearm. Wait. Maybe they are forearm bones. What are those called? The radius and the ulna? Okay, this is not the time to worry what various parts of anatomy are called. You clench one in each hand. And then, you reach as high as you can, and you shove the bone in the dirt of the wall. It catches and you pull up on it. You slam the other bones into the wall, and slowly, six inches at a time, you climb your way out of this pit of death. You're breathing heavy, but you try to be silent as you crest the lip of the pit. And then you are free!

The man and woman don't seem to be around. You set out, looking in each room. You're in some kind of basement. Maybe the basement of the cabin? There's a room at the end of the hall. Slowly you make your way there. And when you get there, you push open the door to horror.

They stand over a table. On it is Hannah. Or what remains of Hannah. There's blood everywhere.

They turn, and you rush forward. And with a solid swing, you thrust one of the bones right through the man's skull. His eyes widen and he collapses to the ground.

There's no time to celebrate. The woman comes at you. The bone is stuck in the man's head, so you let it go, but you still have the other bone. You grasp it and drive it upward through the woman's chin.

"How's that for sittin' purdy?" you say. Then you rush to the table. There is no saving Hannah. But there is saving yourself. You grab a knife from the table, and you find your way outside. Then you run. And you don't stop for anything or anyone until you find civilization.

The police go out. They find your friends . . . in various pieces. Of the five of you, you are the only one left. They question you, and you tell them everything that happened. Then they find you a hotel for the night until you can get a flight out the next day. You don't get a wink of sleep. And as you lay awake for the entire night, you vow to never, not in a million years, ever go camping again.

THE END

You try to put the whole thing behind you. The camping trip. The cave. Your friends who you will never see again. And you try to get back to your normal life. You have a new job lined up, and for the first two weeks, you can almost pretend the entire trip never happened. The job is all-consuming. You drive around neighborhoods and take pictures of homes that are violating the rules of the homeowner's associations. Too many weeds out front. Ugly door colors. Trash cans not put away. It's a bit of a soul sucking job, but you get paid for each violation you find, so you never let one get by.

Two weeks on the job, and your stomach starts hurting. Aching. You snap a picture of a bag of dog poop on the curb, send it to your boss, and then send him an email telling him you're not feeling good. You barely make it home because you're doubled over in pain.

You grab a glass of water, but you can't even take a sip before collapsing on your bedroom floor. You roll onto your back, and your stomach starts to swell. Bigger and bigger. You think about trying to use your cell phone to call 911, but you're in too much pain. Then, as you watch, your stomach splits open. Flesh tears apart. It's half relief from the pressure of your stomach ache and half the worst pain of your life. You try to grab for your phone, just as something crawls out of your stomach. One. Then two. Then twenty. Then hundreds. Little baby cicadas claw their way out from inside you.

They latch onto your exposed skin. They bite through your clothes. And then they begin to feed on you. And as you lay there dying, you realize why the giant cicadas let you go. It was so you could be a host for this: the next generation of cicadas that you're sure will take over the world.

THE END

BEHIND THE SCENES

Hopefully by now you've read this book a bunch of times. You've lived. You've died. What was your favorite death? I personally love the one where baby cicadas grow inside you and finally hatch and feast on your body. Okay, I also love the one where you throw the scarecrow into the fire. Now that is the start of a great camping trip!

Writing interactive adventures is a blast. I love coming up with the various ways things can go wrong. For this one in particular, I loved exploring urban legends. I'd heard the urban legend about the escaped insane asylum patient in the rocking chair since I was in elementary school. Still freaks me out. Also, never pick up hitchhikers.

As with any big project, the first part of starting is planning the project. If you've ever wanted to write your own interactive adventure, I highly recommend you read my book *Write Your Own Quest: The Ultimate Guide to Writing Your Own Interactive Adventure*. I won't go through the process here.

Instead, let's look at the statistics. In *Deady Decisions: Into the Woods,* there are 21 endings. In 9 of those endings, you make it out alive. That means in 12 of those endings, you die. Here's a peak at the story map.

About the Author

P. J. (Tricia) Hoover wanted to be a Jedi, but when that didn't work out, she became an electrical engineer instead. After a fifteen year bout designing computer chips for a living, P. J. started creating worlds of her own. She's the award-winning author of over 30 books, including *Tut: The Story of My Immortal Life*, featuring a fourteen-year-old King Tut who's stuck in middle school, and the editor of *Castle of Horror Volume 6: Femme Fatales*. Under the Connor Hoover pseudonym, she is also the author of the popular *Pick Your Own Quest* series, which are Choose Your Own Adventure style interactive adventures perfect for everyone. When not writing, P. J. loves spending time practicing kung fu, fixing things around the house, and solving Rubik's cubes. For more information about P. J. (Tricia) Hoover, please visit her website www.pjhoover.com.